THE Sarah Jane

ADVENTURES

From the makers of Doctor Who

BBC CHILDREN'S BOOKS

Published by the Penguin Group
Penguin Books Ltd, 80 Strand, London WC2R 0RL, England
Penguin Group (USA) Inc., 375 Hudson Street, New York, New York 10014, USA
Penguin Group (Australia) Ltd, 250 Camberwell Road, Camberwell, Victoria, 3124, Australia
(a division of Pearson Australia Group Pty Ltd)
Canada, India, New Zealand, South Africa

Published by BBC Children's Books, 2007
Text and design © Children's Character Books, 2007

10 9 8 7 6 5 4 3 2 1

Sarah Jane Adventures © BBC 2007

BBC logo ™ & BBC 1996. Licensed by BBC Worldwide Limited

ISBN 978-1-40590-398-1

Printed in the United Kingdom

THE

Sarah Jane
ADVENTURES
From the makers of Doctor Who

Revenge of
the Slitheen

Written by Rupert Laight

Based on the script by Gareth Roberts

'I saw amazing things, out there in space. But there's strangeness to be found wherever you turn. Life on Earth can be an adventure, too.

You just have to know where to look.'

SARAH JANE SMITH

Prologue

'The premises comprise nine offices, three storage rooms and a large open-plan warehouse,' explained Janine, the estate agent, as she showed an overweight man with a red face and greying hair round the dingy industrial unit. 'What kind of business were you intending to use it for?'

'Business?' The man rubbed his leg as if he was in discomfort. 'Oh, this and that. Y'know – construction, development.' He paused, grinning. 'World domination.'

Not being the brightest of sparks, Janine wondered how to react. 'Sorry?' she managed.

'Only having a laugh, my dear,' said the man. But he wasn't laughing.

Janine was twenty-eight years old and out

of shape. She was unhappy with her size and unhappy with her job. She'd never set out to be an estate agent, but it was the best money she could earn in the area, considering her lack of qualifications and experience.

'Anyway,' she continued, trying to change the subject, 'the area offers excellent transport links, low council tax, and a large local workforce.'

'That's good, because I need to recruit a...um... *very large* workforce.' The man gave a smug smile, as if enjoying a private joke.

'Really?' Janine raised an eyebrow. 'What kind of people are you planning to take on?' She ventured, testing the water.

The man considered for a moment. He looked her up and down. She was a hefty, lumpen thing wearing a faded grey trouser suit a size too small for her. But at least she'd be roomy. Yes, she'd do very nicely. 'Is that a hint, my dear?'

'Er, well, no, I was just...' Janine trailed off, embarrassed.

'I see,' he mused, shifting awkwardly and stretching an arm. 'You'd like to join us?' He smiled that self-satisfied smile again. 'Yes, maybe you could be of use.'

'Really?' Janine's face lit up.

'You're just the right...' the man searched for an appropriate word.

'Kind of employee you're looking for?' offered Janine.

'Just the right... *siiiiiize!*'

And before Janine could ask what he meant, she was bathed in a shocking bright light that made her cover her eyes and turn her head away.

The last thing she heard was a strange, gurgling voice, like the man's, but somehow different, almost alien...

'That's right, my dear, you're just the ticket. My sister needs a new body.' The voice broke into a terrifying chortle. 'The family's back – and they're hungry. Hungry for *revenge!*'

Chapter One

Food for thought

Sunday evenings are always a drag, but this particular Sunday was a bigger drag than usual.

Maria Jackson had to go to school in the morning. What's more, it was the first day of term. And if things could get worse – which they always could – she was starting at a new school.

Maria sighed and looked out of her bedroom window. It was raining. But through the sodden haze she could still make out Sarah Jane Smith's house.

Number thirteen Bannerman Road was different to the new, grey, two-storey house she lived in with

H 4 T R F G 8 N D 1 S W O B X O 3 T R 2 U F S 7 K

her dad. It stood alone behind a high red-brick wall. It was large, Victorian and, if she didn't know better, rather creepy-looking.

Maria had only recently come to the area. Her parents had split up a year ago, and her mum had gone to live with her new fella. But she wasn't complaining. She'd always got on better with her dad. He understood her – as best as a dad could, anyway.

She'd made a new friend, too. Sarah Jane may have been several times the age of her old mates, but she was a hundred times cooler. After all, no one else Maria knew was on first-name terms with creatures from outer space.

Thinking back over the past few days, Maria smiled to herself. She'd had an amazing time. She'd met real-life aliens and foiled a plot to enslave humanity. So much better than hanging out at the shopping centre, or reading magazines about celebrities.

But was that adventure to be just a one-off? Might the story be over now? Maria wanted more. It had whetted her appetite for the unexpected, the dangerous. She felt depressed to think alien-bashing could be only a passing phase, like playing with dolls. Was all that weirdness really behind her?

Maria needn't have worried...

Park Vale School was only a ten-minute walk from Bannerman Road, and Maria was early. She paused outside the gates to gather her thoughts before facing the barrage of new faces.

As she leaned against the brickwork, a stylish, pale green car pulled up, the driver's door swung open, and out stepped Sarah Jane Smith.

Luke slipped out from the passenger seat.

Sarah lazily ran a hand through her shoulder-length auburn hair. She was slim and pretty, with a touch of real glamour that appealed to Maria. The clothes she wore were sophisticated yet somehow girly. Though middle-aged, she still had a mass of untapped energy. She clearly hadn't finished with being young, even if it had finished with her.

'You take care,' she said to Luke, with an earnest smile.

'Goodbye...Mum,' he replied.

'Mum? Don't think so. Sarah Jane's just fine.' Glancing around, she noticed Maria smiling over. 'Hi, Maria.'

Maria watched as Sarah Jane leaned over and planted a kiss on Luke's cheek, then climbed back into the car and drove off. She always seemed to be in a hurry, as if she was permanently late for an appointment.

A group of nearby boys started to laugh.

'Why are they doing that?' Luke asked Maria, confused.

Luke had been born yesterday. Well, not yesterday exactly, but only a couple of months ago. And he hadn't exactly been born either. He'd been built – like you build a computer – by an alien race called the Bane. But when they built him, even though they made him really brainy, they forgot to install any guidelines for being human. He didn't have a clue how mere mortals behave.

'First day and your mum's kissing you goodbye,' explained Maria.

'Is that bad?'

'Bit embarrassing.' She paused. 'And I got the feeling she wanted you to call her Mum.'

Luke frowned. 'She said she didn't.'

'It's not what she said, more how she said it.' But Luke didn't get it.

They headed through the school gates and into the playground. Looking up, Maria took in the grey and white Sixties building. Then her gaze was pulled to the left, where a squeaky-clean new block stood. It looked out of place, like it had been delivered to the wrong address.

'That's a bit flashy,' she said.

'It's a brand new building,' explained Luke. 'There was an article about it in the newspaper.'

'So what's inside?'

Luke shrugged.

On a post in the playground a CCTV camera followed Maria and Luke as they headed in for assembly...

'Not them. Scan along,' said a gruff male voice.

Luke and Maria were being watched on an oddly-shaped monitor. The camera slid past them and over groups of kids enjoying their final moments before the bell rang.

'Where is he?' demanded another voice, impatiently. This one sounded oddly sinister and distant.

'There!'

The image came to a sudden stop on Mr Jeffrey, a chubby science teacher in his mid-thirties, carrying a battered leather briefcase. He had a disappointed expression on his face, like his life hadn't turned out the way he'd planned.

'He's not that big. How will I fit?'

'He'll do. Get yourself ready.'

The gruff-voiced man beamed menacingly. It was Mr Blakeman, the headmaster.

'What can I do for you, Greg?' asked Mr Jeffrey, nervously. He wondered what he'd done wrong so early in the term.

'I need you to stand right there, Tim.'

They had been walking down a corridor in the new block, Blakeman leading the way. The corridor ended with a blank, white wall. Blakeman moved his colleague around until his back was against it.

'Any particular reason?' enquired Mr Jeffrey.

'Very particular.'

And then the headmaster did something unusual. *Phaaaaarzzze!* He let out a tremendous, wall-rattling fart. Not what you expect from a grown-up. More what little boys impress their mates with.

Mr Jeffrey's jaw dropped. 'Happens to us all,' he managed, more to fill the silence than to offer an explanation.

Blakeman ignored him. 'I'll need that,' he said, pointing at the science teacher's briefcase.

'Sorry?' Mr Jeffrey was puzzled, but the head's tone of authority made him loosen his grip, and the case was pulled from his hand.

Behind him, the wall slid silently open. The headmaster smirked.

A huge, green, three-fingered hand with long, glinting talons appeared in the opening and gently settled on Jeffrey's unsuspecting shoulder. The teacher spun round.

'Aaaaaaargh!'

But his scream was cut short, as the claw's grip tightened around his neck...

On a bench in the school hall, Luke and Maria sat shyly glancing around at their new schoolmates.

It was assembly, and the packed, airless room was filled with the hum of chatter. Teachers were seating themselves on the stage, doing teacher-ish things, like discussing the curriculum or drawing up lesson plans.

'I'm feeling anxious.' It was Luke's first day at Park Vale, too.

'So am I,' said Maria.

'But you've been to school before.'

'Not this one.'

'Does that matter?' asked Luke, trying to understand.

A boy bashed into Maria's side. 'Budge up!' he demanded, and plonked himself down next to her. 'You new today?'

'Yep,' said Maria, and introduced herself.

'I'm Clyde,' replied the boy, looking straight ahead. He was a tall, good-looking lad, with an easy, self-assured manner. 'New, too. Probably hang round with you till I meet some cooler people.'

'Charming!' snorted Maria.

'How do you do?' Luke extended a hand. 'I'm Luke Smith.'

'That was a joke,' said Clyde, ignoring the hand. 'But now I mean it.'

A hush had fallen over the hall and all eyes had

turned forward. The headmaster had taken his position at the centre of the stage.

He was a tall, overweight man, with thinning hair and a self-satisfied expression plastered across his face. He clearly enjoyed being a headmaster – it gave him power.

'Good morning, everyone,' he boomed.

'Gooooood moooorning, Miiiister Blaaakemaaan,' the kids droned in unison.

There was silence as Blakeman squirmed. He gripped hold of his backside and adjusted himself. It was as if his underwear was too tight. And then there was a gurgling, rumbling noise, like his stomach was seriously upset. *Phaaaaarzzze!* He emitted a thundering bottom burp.

Stunned silence. Then the school dissolved into laughter.

'What's funny?' demanded the head. 'My wife made me cheese and bean tartlets last night.' Then under his breath, 'Another reason to despise Jamie Oliver.'

Maria frowned. This never happened at her last school.

'Right. Assembly. Ya-de-dah.' Blakeman seemed bored. 'Welcome back. It's a new year. Hope you all do well. Erm...' He paused, as if he was unsure what to say next. 'Don't run in the courtyard, don't even think about wearing make-up, and study hard, because I guarantee that none of you are going to be pop stars.'

'What's his problem?' whispered Clyde.

Just then Mr Jeffrey climbed the steps of the stage. He too wriggled uncomfortably as he seated himself near the headmaster. Were everyone's underpants irritating them this morning?

'So, what else? Oh yeah...' Blakeman smirked. 'What a bright future you've all got, children of the world...etcetera, etcetera,' he added, in a sinister tone, and glanced at Jeffrey. 'As you've seen, we've got a new technology block. I'm taking you over in groups for a look around at the amazing facilities. Starting with class 10B.'

That was Luke and Clyde's form.

The foyer of the new block was as white as a hospital sheet, and as plain as the most minimal of modern buildings. It had no homeliness or comfort to it. It seemed as if it was there only to function, to exist, not to stimulate or inspire.

Luke, Clyde and their classmates looked around them, not sure whether to be impressed or intimidated.

'There are sixteen classrooms, three of which are dedicated computer rooms, fully equipped with broadband wireless Internet connections,' informed the headmaster. 'But anything *untoward* your adolescent minds might be drawn to on the Internet, I've locked out.'

Blakeman continued his introductory talk as he moved out into a corridor, and the class followed him. Luke and Clyde shuffled along at the back.

'I've signed up for the lunchtime Science Club,' Luke announced, proud of himself. 'First meeting's tomorrow.'

'Now I'm backing away,' muttered Clyde.

Luke didn't get a chance to defend himself as, just then, Blakeman let out another noisy expulsion of wind. Form 10B fell about. This was getting to be a habit.

'Shut up!' he bellowed.

'Why is farting funny?' wondered Luke aloud.

Clyde's brow furrowed. 'It just is.'

'But it's a normal process of the human bowel.'

'Are you for real?' asked Clyde, sarcastically. And then he sniffed the air. 'Smells weird in here.'

'Farts?'

Clyde shook his head. 'It's...dunno...metal, electric.'

'Like batteries,' offered Luke, catching a whiff of the strange aroma in the new block.

The boys stared at one another. What was it?

Maria distractedly pushed her food around the plate. It was lunchtime and the canteen was packed. Clyde plonked himself on the seat next to her, and let his plate of shepherd's pie clank down on to the table. 'Can I sit here?'

'Only if I'm not gonna shame you,' replied Maria, haughtily.

'Well, I either sit here with you, or sit there with *that*.' He indicated the only other free seat, next to an overweight, nerdy boy a year or two younger than them.

'What – there's someone worse than me?'

'Just,' said Clyde. But he didn't really mean it.

'So where are you from?' asked Maria.

'Hounslow. My folks split up. I moved here with my mum.'

'That's like me. Only I moved with my dad.'

The pair smiled at one another. Then Clyde looked away. 'How's that for you?' he asked, coolly. He had to maintain his public image.

'Better than when they were rowing all the time.'

Clyde nodded an agreement and went to put a forkful of food into his mouth. The fork froze in midair. He stared down at the shepherd's pie. It was mottled with mould.

'Look at that!' he cried, horrified. 'What kind of slop are they serving here? Leftovers from last term or something?' Clyde shoved the fork through his food. It was full of revolting green, blue and grey furry patches. Totally inedible.

'Mr Blakeman!' he called, attracting the head's attention as he passed through the canteen.

'What?' snapped Blakeman.

'Look at this.' Clyde tipped the plate so he could see. 'How am I supposed to eat that?'

'Just pick out the bad bits,' replied Blakeman airily, and he moved off, humming to himself. It was as if he didn't care. Or he wasn't surprised.

'Huh!' grunted Clyde. 'That leaves me with one pea.'

Maria was glad she'd chosen a salad. But then she looked closer. 'Mine's off too! It's disgusting!'

They stared at one another in disbelief.

'What's wrong with this place? It stinks of electric, the food's rotten...' Clyde trailed off. 'There's something *really* weird going on here.'

Chapter Two

Behind the secret door

The school day was over. The last of the children were heading off home or hanging around the gates waiting for parents to pick them up, or just chatting with their mates.

Mr Blakeman and Mr Jeffrey stood side-by-side in the foyer surveying the dawdlers through the window.

'Goodbye, repellent pubescents.' The head's false smile turned into a very real frown. 'Until tomorrow.'

Jeffrey wriggled uncomfortably and rubbed his thighs. 'This skin. It's killing me round the legs.'

Blakeman ignored him. 'Right. Time for a test

run,' he announced, rubbing his hands together with glee.

'Now?' queried his colleague. 'What about the caretaker?'

'I've taken care of the caretaker,' the head replied, chuckling at his own cleverness. 'At last, everything is ready. Come on!'

A car pulled up outside number thirteen Bannerman Road. It was Sarah Jane's car. Her passengers, Luke and Maria, got out, followed by Sarah herself.

Then another car pulled up directly across the road at number twelve. It was Maria's dad, Alan Jackson. He was back from work early.

'I see you've cadged a lift,' he called to Maria as he got out.

Sarah Jane replied on her behalf. 'I offered.'

'I dunno,' sighed Alan. 'Lady Muck – getting the neighbours to chauffeur her about!'

'Shut up, Dad!' said Maria, jokingly.

'So, how was your first day then?' asked Alan.

'Okay...' But there was something Maria wanted to say. 'It's a bit weird though,' she ventured. 'The headmaster doesn't seem to want to be there.' She paused, wondering how her next words would sound. 'And he keeps...farting.'

'What – noisy, smelly ones?' joked Alan.

'Or silent-but-deadlies?'

'Both. It was like he'd had three biryanis the night before.'

'The place stinks of batteries, too,' added Luke. 'And the canteen food was off.'

'I'll make you a proper tea,' said Sarah to the lad, and she gestured towards their front door.

'Bye,' called Luke, then went inside.

'I want a proper tea, too,' demanded Maria, with a playful smile.

'Make it yourself,' teased her dad. 'Sarah Jane may be your chauffeur, but I'm not your cook!'

'Dad!' protested Maria, and she headed over the road to her own house. Sarah Jane and Alan were left alone.

'Well, the school can't be that bad. They just built this.' She took out the local newspaper from her bag.

On page three was an article about Park Vale, with a cheesy photo of Blakeman pointing at the new block – in case you might accidentally miss it.

'This new technology centre was put up over the holidays,' said Sarah. 'Someone donated the money. Looks incredible.'

Alan was thinking. 'I did an IT job at a school. It was in a new block that looked exactly like that one.' He paused. 'Now I think about it, that placed smelt odd, too. Kind of electrical.'

'Like batteries?'

'Sort of. Plus, if you took sandwiches in, they'd be off by lunchtime.'

Sarah Jane was studying the report. If her brain had been a clock, you would have heard the ticking speed up. She was making connections most of us would see as coincidence. 'Was it built by Coldfire Construction?'

Alan nodded.

'Where was that?'

'Other side of town. St Cheldon's, in Upminster.'

Maria stuck her head round the front door and called across to her dad. 'What d'ya want for tea then?'

'Forget it. We'll phone for a curry. Can't have you straining yourself after your long journey home.' He gave her a knowing wink.

'Think you're so funny, don't you?' Maria stuck her tongue out playfully and disappeared back inside the house.

Sarah Jane noted their easy relationship with one another. Though she'd chosen to look after Luke when he'd escaped the Bane, having had no kids of her own, she was unsure how it all worked. It was one of the few things in life she was unsure about.

'How did you get like that – you and Maria?' she asked, trying not to sound jealous.

'It's always been like this,' he replied, shrugging. 'Don't really think about it.'

Sarah Jane smiled sadly and went inside.

In a concealed room within the new block at Park Vale School, Blakeman and Jeffrey were putting their twisted plan into action.

In front of them was a control panel. But it was nothing like they'd ever seen before – not even on the latest mobile phone, or the most up-to-date computer. It was comfortably old-fashioned, as if everything had been made easy to use, with levers and knobs instead of flashing lights and touch-operated displays. Yet it was also incredibly high-tech.

This was alien technology.

Jeffrey pushed a lever away from him and, as he did so, a low hum began, like the sound of a fridge. However, this hum was gradually growing louder and louder...

'That's it,' said Blakeman, light flashing across his bloated features. 'Now synchronise the mega-wattage.'

Jeffrey scanned the panel for the correct switch.

'That one!' boomed the headmaster.

'Erm...' Mr Jeffrey scratched his head.

'Oh, I'll do it myself!'

Blakeman flicked a seemingly insignificant switch. The hum doubled in volume and climbed the scale to a high-pitched whine. Smoke started to fill the room. Sparks crackled around the edges of the machine.

The capacitor was powering up...

Sarah Jane's study in the attic of thirteen Bannerman Road was a magical place. It was cluttered with bits and pieces of alien technology that its owner had gathered from her travels. Yet it still felt homely – a playroom for a grown-up. It was Sarah Jane's den, her refuge, and the place in the world where she felt safest.

On the shelves and tacked to the walls were photos from Sarah Jane's travels – the Brigadier, whom she'd once worked with at UNIT. Harry Sullivan, another old friend of the Doctor's. A sketch of a Dalek. A picture of her and K-9 at Morton Harewood. These were all things that no one but her closest friends were allowed to see.

Sarah Jane was sat at her computer, scrolling through lists of results the search engine had spewed out. Her notebook was lying open on the table beside her. To an untrained eye her notes would have made no sense, but Sarah Jane had her own way of doing things.

'I kept making social mistakes today.' Luke had quietly entered the room.

Sarah Jane carried on looking at the screen. 'I think I made one too – driving you to school when it's just round the corner. Then kissing you goodbye.' Sarah Jane spoke to Luke like she would an adult. 'We're both new hands at this.'

'I don't know anybody except Maria and Clyde,' explained Luke. 'Maria's in different classes to me most of the time. And Clyde thinks I'm uncool.'

'Clyde's not the only kid in the school.'

'What if I make more mistakes?'

'Then you'll never make the same ones again.' Sarah Jane felt she was starting to get the hang of this 'mother' thing. 'Listen, anyone's nervous starting a new school, a new job, a new...' She stopped, remembering the time when she first travelled with the Doctor. But that wasn't a good example.

'I've never been a mum before,' she offered instead.

Luke sighed. 'Do I have to go?'

Sarah Jane gave what she hoped was a reassuring smile. 'I could take you out of school and teach you myself. I considered it.' She took Luke's hand. 'But you, Luke Smith, you're going to live a normal life. As normal a life as I can give you.' Deep down, however, Sarah Jane knew life would never be normal when she was around, but she had to reassure him somehow. 'All the rules, making friends, reading the signals – it just happens.'

'What if I get it wrong again?' said Luke. 'It makes me feel stupid.'

'Remember,' said Sarah Jane, and she looked her new-found son in the eye as she spoke, 'you saved the world on the day you were born. Not many people can say that.'

'*Nobody* else can say that.' Luke looked away. 'And that's the problem. Nobody else is like me.'

Sarah Jane didn't know what to say. She just smiled, then gently let go of his hand and turned back to the computer.

'What are you looking for?' Luke asked, his natural curiosity getting the better of him.

'Checking up on the firm that built your new school block.' Sarah Jane glanced at her notebook. 'They're called Coldfire Construction. They started expanding eighteen months ago. Contracts all round the world. Some odd things cropping up.'

She fell silent, her eyes narrowed in thought. 'Now they're putting up school buildings all round London.' Sarah Jane chuckled to herself. 'Makes a change for me. At least it's not aliens!'

But she couldn't have been more wrong...

Chapter Three

'Lights out, London!'

'Only me!' declared a loud voice. Maria's mum, Chrissie, was a woman who liked to make her presence felt. 'I've come for a gawp.' She was also painfully honest.

Alan was brushed to one side as his former wife barged her way through the front door and down the hallway.

Once in the living room, Chrissie fell silent – which didn't happen often – coolly appraising the decor and furnishings. 'Well, you've got it looking kind of all right,' she admitted, begrudgingly.

'Thanks. I really value your opinion,' added Alan, sarcastically.

Chrissie ignored him. 'Maria upstairs?'

'Yeah. It seemed to go okay for her today.'

'What went okay?'

'Her first day – at a new school.'

For a moment, Alan had forgotten how thoughtless Chrissie could be, but this brought it all back. How could he ever have believed their marriage would work?

'Was that today?' she asked. 'My mind's been all over the place. Stress you would not believe – '

Chrissie would have gone on, but Alan cut in. 'So why did you come round?'

'To see my daughter, Alan,' she replied, sharply. 'Do I need any other reason? Though now I think, you were gonna give me that double duvet.' She headed out into the hall. 'You don't need it, you've got the single.'

Alan sighed. Did he have a choice?

'Maria, love!' she called. 'It's your mum!'

Mr Jeffrey and Mr Blakeman stared at the light coming from their machinery. As they did so, the sound that had once been a hum was becoming a loud, intense rumbling. The sparks and smoke the equipment was emitting increased in ferocity.

Jeffrey threw another lever on the control panel. 'There!' he said, triumphant.

Blakeman let out a sinister, self-satisfied laugh. 'Lights out, London!' he said.

Chrissie, Alan and Maria were sitting in the lounge.

'The school can't be that bad,' Chrissie told Maria. 'This is a better catchment area.' She looked at her watch. 'I can't stop long. Ivan's taking me to the pub. It's opera night. The waiters sing while you're eating.'

Now she lived with her dad, Maria hardly saw her mum. It wasn't just that they now lived quite far apart, it was also due to the fact that Ivan had come onto the scene. Ivan was Chrissie's boyfriend.

Maria was just about to ask her mum to stay on a little longer, when every light at number twelve Bannerman Road suddenly went out.

'Great,' said Alan, frowning.

'There's a torch,' offered Maria, and she fetched it from the sideboard. She pushed the 'on' switch. For a moment it lit up, but quickly faded to blackness.

'With a flat battery,' said Chrissie, unhelpfully.

Alan sighed.

'I'm not saying anything,' huffed Chrissie.

'I'll get the candles,' he said.

Over the road, number thirteen was dark too. Sarah Jane was searching through a drawer.

'Power cut?' Luke asked.

Sarah Jane nodded. 'The computer went pffft, and guess who forgot to save her work...'

She found what she was looking for. A torch. But when she turned it on, it went straight off again.

'Oh, great,' said Sarah Jane. Then she remembered, and glanced at her watch. But it wasn't the time she was interested in.

She flipped open the face to reveal her scanner. The Doctor had given it to her. He'd assembled it using technology from beyond the stars. It could help detect aliens and do all sorts of things a normal watch couldn't.

'I'll see how long it's gonna be,' continued Sarah Jane. 'I can check the local power grid on my...' But she trailed off. The scanner watch was dead. Sarah Jane was flabbergasted. 'That's impossible. It never loses power.' She paused, staring at Luke. 'It *can't* lose power.'

Alan brought the candles through from the kitchen. 'There we go,' he said.

Chrissie was looking out the window into the darkened street. There wasn't a glimmer of man-made light to be seen. For once, you could appreciate the stars in their full glory.

'Goes as far as I can see,' she noted. 'Used to happen all the time when I was a kid. And always when there was something good on the telly.' She smiled to herself. 'Went off right in the middle of *Manimal* once. I was distraught.'

Alan lit the candle, but it too went out – as if it was powered by electricity and the plug had been pulled out. His jaw dropped in astonishment.

He tried another, just in case. The same thing happened.

'That's *so* weird,' said Maria, perplexed. 'Why's that happening? Are they wet?'

'No,' replied her dad.

'Give 'em here!' demanded Chrissie, snatching the box from Alan. If anyone could force a candle to light, it was her!

'What was that?' asked Jeffrey.

Their machine was making a terrifying grinding sound and producing so much smoke it was hard to see Blakeman through the fug. It was straining at the very limit of its capacity. Something would blow at any moment.

'It's destabilised!' cried the headmaster, losing his cool.

'Switch it off!' screamed his colleague. 'Switch it off!'

Blakeman reversed the lever...

All of a sudden, Sarah Jane's watch came back to life. And as it did, the attic was once again lit up, the computer started to reboot and the torch switched itself on.

Chrissie had snatched the candle from Alan and was lighting it. This one stayed lit.

'There!' she said, triumphant.

Just then the other candles that Alan had attempted to light flickered into a steady flame – like those birthday candles that can't be blown out.

Maria gasped. This was so bizarre.

'Weird,' said Sarah Jane, looking at her watch.

'It must be faulty,' offered Luke.

Sarah Jane shook her head. She wasn't convinced. The watch had never let her down before. There was more to this than met the eye. Then she had a brainwave. 'Or the same thing that cut the electric off, and cut the torch off...'

'Cut your watch off.' Luke was making the connection, too.

'Fantastic!' said Jeffrey, as they headed down the shiny white corridor of the new block. 'Finally, every station in the loop is working.' He frowned. 'But the stabiliser cuts out.'

'I'll work out how to fix it,' reassured Blakeman.

But Jeffrey was cross with his colleague. '*You* bought those plans off that Wallarian,' he complained. '*You* took his word it worked.'

'I just need to sort out the storage problem. Then it'll stabilise.'

'And until then I'm stuck here in this!' snorted Jeffrey, indicating his clumsy human form. 'Teaching science on Planet Thick! They still haven't worked out String Theory!'

'Can it!' barked Blakeman, sick of Jeffrey's complaints. 'Don't you get it? We're nearly there!' He turned, folded his arms and smiled. 'One more step – and then we will destroy this planet!'

Chapter Four

The offending chip butty

S arah Jane looked up at the sky. It was Tuesday morning and overcast. Heavy grey clouds gave the day a sinister, foreboding feel, and there was a distinct chill in the air.

She searched in her handbag for the car keys. Then she paused and looked across the road at number twelve – an idea forming...

'Science is my first class today,' said a despondent Luke, closing the front door behind him. He was neatly dressed in his school uniform. 'Lab 2A, with Mr Jeffrey.'

Sarah Jane tried to sound casual. She didn't want to make a bigger deal out of it than was necessary. 'You'll be fine,' she said, and headed over the road. 'See you later.'

Luke stared after her. What was she up to? Then he shrugged and started off for school.

Sarah Jane made her way down the side of the house and into the back garden. Alan was digging a flowerbed.

'Hi there,' she said. 'Not interrupting, am I?'

'No,' replied Alan, and he dug the fork into the soil, dusted off his hands and smiled at his neighbour. 'Just making a start. Used to have a much bigger garden. Back at the old house.'

'Do you miss it?' asked Sarah Jane, always the inquisitive journalist.

'Well, needs must,' said Alan, clearly attempting to sound cheerful. 'New life and all that.' He smiled thinly. 'I had all sorts of plans for that old garden. Just didn't plan on my wife running off with a judo instructor.' He paused. 'Ever been married?'

'No,' said Sarah Jane, shaking her head. 'Never found the time.'

'Wise move. Anyway, sorry. You were saying?'

'Yes...' Her eyes narrowed in thought. 'I was just wondering. That school you mentioned. In

Upminster. St Cheldon's?'

Alan nodded.

'Do you have any paperwork or plans of the new block they built?'

'I think so,' he said. 'Follow me.' And he led Sarah Jane in through the back door. 'I won't be a sec.'

Alan disappeared off down the hallway, leaving Sarah Jane to examine the kitchen, which was dominated by an enormous stack of dirty plates, and boxes of pans and crockery that had yet to be unpacked.

A few minutes later he returned with a brown folder filled with pieces of paper. 'Here we go.' He teased out a folded sheet and opened it on the counter. It was an architect's drawing of the block. 'Cost a fortune. They had broadband installed, the works.'

'Where did the money come from?'

'Dunno. Private funding?' Alan looked at Sarah Jane with curiosity. 'What sort of journalist are you exactly?'

'Oh, this and that,' shrugged Sarah Jane, innocently. 'Local stories – nothing exciting.'

'Maria was saying you'd travelled a fair bit.'

'You could say that...' Sarah Jane gave a melancholy smile, thinking off all her adventures in the TARDIS.

'What's that area?' she asked, pointing at the plans. 'It's blank.'

'Never went in. Coldfire kept that to themselves. It was all sealed off.'

'But there's no door,' frowned Sarah.

'What – do you think they're hiding something?'

'Inside a school?' She smiled, not wanting Maria's dad to think her insane. 'That would be ridiculous, wouldn't it?'

'Just a bit.'

There was an awkward silence.

'Do you mind if I keep this?' asked Sarah Jane.

'Help yourself.'

She folded the plan and slipped it into her bag.

'A transformer is an electrical device that changes the voltage of an alternating current supply, the AC supply,' said Mr Jeffrey in a bored tone.

It was Science and Luke was listening attentively. Next to him sat Clyde. He was staring at a fair-haired girl on the next bench and fidgeting in his chair.

The lab was tatty, the worktops carved with the graffiti of three decades of bored pupils, the varnish almost entirely worn away. In front of the whiteboard and behind a large drawerless desk, stood Mr Jeffrey.

But this wasn't the nervous, fidgeting Jeffrey the pupils had come to know and loathe. A change had come over the science teacher, leaving him short-tempered, arrogant and prone to violent attacks of wind.

'Of course, transformers are a vital part of your...' – he corrected himself – '*our* mains electrical supply. Anyone know who invented the first transformer?'

Luke's hand immediately shot up. Jeffrey nodded in his direction.

'Faraday,' said Luke, knowing he was right.

'Correct.'

'Though he didn't realise what you could use it for,' added the boy.

His words were met with 'Oohs' and 'Get yous' from the rest of the class, stunned at the new kid's eagerness to please. It was deeply uncool.

'What?' said Jeffrey, surprised. He hadn't imagined the human young could be so intelligent.

'Faraday didn't know what he'd invented,' continued Luke. 'I've thought about it, too. You could get rid of transformers, get a better system and induct power instead.'

The science teacher had to stop his mouth from falling open. Was this child for real?

At the same time, Clyde buried his head in his hands. This was so embarrassing. 'Just pointing out,' he said to the class, 'I'm nothing to do with him.'

Everyone started to laugh. Luke felt his cheeks burn. He'd done it again – made a fool of himself. How was he meant to understand what things were cool to know about and what things were... what was the word Maria had used...nerdy?

Mr Jeffrey banged his fist on the desk. 'Quiet!'

The room fell silent. All eyes on Clyde.

'Name!' demanded the teacher.

'Clyde Langer.'

'Troublemaker. Noted.' Jeffrey looked back down at the textbook on his desk.

Clyde couldn't hide his grin. He liked being branded a troublemaker. 'Okay,' he said and smiled round at the rest of the class. The girl he'd been looking at earlier smiled back.

Luke was figuring it all out – why his new friend got it so right and he got it so very wrong. 'Okay,' he mused. 'Clyde's cool because he makes trouble.' A pause, then a thought came to him. 'Should I make trouble, too?' he said out loud.

'I hear talking,' said Mr Jeffrey, without looking up.

Total silence – broken only when Clyde started rummaging around in a carrier bag he'd brought with him. He took out a sweet and popped it into his mouth.

'What are you doing?' demanded the teacher, who seemed now to never miss a thing.

'My pen's run out,' lied Clyde. 'I'm getting a new one.'

But Mr Jeffrey wasn't fooled. 'Let me see that!' And he picked up a huge pair of lab tongs and marched over to Clyde. Picking up the plastic bag, he sniffed cautiously at it. His face immediately turned pale, like he was about to be sick. 'What's in here?'

'Just my lunch,' he replied, defensively. 'Chip butty. Made it meself. Not chancing my life in that canteen again.'

Holding the bag at arm's length, Jeffrey made for the nearest window, flung it open and launched the carrier out. The class stared, aghast.

'Oi!' protested Clyde. 'You can't do that! Who d'ya think you are?'

'You can use the canteen like everyone else.'

'I'll report you for that!'

'Go on,' said the teacher, leaning in close to Clyde. 'Just try it,' he threatened. And then a deep churning sound and...*Phaaaaarzzze!* He let out a belter – to rival even the headmaster's.

The class started laughing, but Jeffrey clearly wasn't amused.

It was just then that the bell rang.

'Right,' said Jeffrey. 'For tomorrow – 1,000 words

on transformers. No. Make it 2,000.'

And as the pupils packed up, muttering about the many injustices of teenage life, Mr Jeffrey gave Luke a long, curious stare...

St Cheldon's Comprehensive School in Upminster was an imposing Victorian building. Its brick, once red, had turned a dull brown, and the paint was peeling on the window frames. There was graffiti over the front wall, and the playground had cracks in its tarmac where weeds poked through.

Sarah Jane Smith got out of her car and stared up. This was similar to the kind of place she'd been to school. But that had been in Liverpool, and more years ago than she cared to remember.

So, where's this new block? she wondered to herself. Must be round the back.

It was. And it looked exactly the same as the one at Luke and Maria's school.

Sarah couldn't help speculating why someone would spend all this money on a new block, when the old one was falling apart. It didn't make sense.

'It's hopeless, Miss Smith,' said Wendy, the headmistress, as they descended the stairs. 'Even worse this term.'

Wendy was a disheartened-looking woman in

her mid-fifties. She was thin, pale and dressed in dark blues and browns. She carried a large leather bag over one shoulder.

'I believe you had the wiring in your new block reinstalled?'

Wendy sighed. 'Didn't do any good. The computers still keep crashing. And look at this.' She produced an apple from her bag. It was covered in mould. 'Fresh this morning. Everything goes off.' She paused. 'And there's that smell. Like batteries.'

'And this all started when you got your new technology centre?' Sarah Jane frowned. 'Doesn't anybody care? Hasn't anyone tried to work out what's wrong?'

'One of the parent governors raised it at our meeting.'

'And?'

'He fell off his bike the next morning. Three months in traction. Do you think that's a coincidence?'

Sarah Jane shook her head. This was more serious than she'd imagined. Someone didn't like these new school blocks being investigated. Perhaps there was an 'accident' already planned for her. She made a promise to herself to tread carefully.

Realising they'd reached the end of their

conversation, Sarah shook the headmistress's hand.

'Can't you feel it?' Wendy lowered her voice to a whisper.

'Sorry?' said Sarah Jane.

'Like a thunderstorm's coming.'

In another room, in another part of the city, a podgy-fingered female hand flicked off the screen on which she had been observing this conversation. The hand belonged to Janine, the estate agent.

At least, it looked like Janine...

Back at Park Vale, Mr Jeffrey was talking to the headmaster about Luke. 'Incredible knowledge. This child...' He paused to consider. 'He must be a freak.'

'You really think he could help us?' asked Blakeman.

'Yes. We'll use him to solve the storage problem.'

The head couldn't believe it. 'A fourteen-year-old child?'

'There's something strange about him,' said Jeffrey, in hushed tones. 'These kids stink. Acne and grease and coats and crisps. But he smells... fresh.'

'When can you get to him?'

'Very soon,' he smirked. 'We've got an appointment...'

The science lab was a totally different place at lunchtime. The only sound in the room was the distant shouts and excited screams of the schoolchildren in the playground.

'Welcome to our Science Club,' said Mr Jeffrey. He was standing at the front of the class. 'I'd hoped for a higher turnout, but never mind.'

Luke sat alone, listening politely to the teacher. 'It's just me,' he said, a little sheepishly.

'And me!' a loud voice announced. And in walked Carl. He introduced himself to Luke and sat down next to him.

'Pleased to meet you,' said Luke. He looked the twelve-year-old up and down. He was plain and rather overweight, his hair was greasy and his shoes were scuffed. But he had a friendly face, and Luke felt pleased that he wasn't the only boy in the school opting for extra classes. It made him feel part of a team. Albeit a small one.

'Carl's the science star of the school,' Mr Jeffrey announced. 'Supposedly,' he added, with an eyebrow raised. 'Though I think he's probably pretty rubbish compared to you.'

Embarrassed at the flattery, Luke glanced at Carl. The lad looked deflated.

'Now,' continued Mr Jeffrey, regardless, 'over the summer I've been having tons of jolly fun working on a new project. Take a look at this.' He switched on a lightbox with a sheet of acetate on it. Luke and Carl craned forward to get a better look.

What they saw was a very complicated diagram. A huge, interwoven electrical circuit.

'What do you make of it?' he asked.

'Er...' Carl scratched his head.

'It's a model for a giant capacitor system,' said Luke, brightening up.

'And purely theoretical, of course,' added Mr Jeffrey, quickly. 'Nobody could possibly build anything like this for real.'

'Did you really design that?' asked Luke.

'Oh yes. I'm wasted here,' the teacher replied. 'Do you like it?'

'It's amazing. Let me have a look.' Luke studied the diagram. A fascinated grin was spreading across his face. This was the kind of thing he loved.

'But I've got a problem,' frowned Jeffrey. 'My *purely theoretical* problem,' and he made a special effort to emphasise these words, 'is...' He trailed off, and threw the floor open to Carl and Luke. 'Anyone?'

'Don't tell me,' blurted out Luke, excitedly. 'Oh yeah! With this you could store huge amounts of electrical energy.' He paused. 'But there's a loophole here in the storage. It wouldn't stabilise.'

The teacher's eyes lit up. This kid was brighter than even he had hoped. 'Well done! Gold star! That's my problem.' He turned to Carl. 'No star,' he said, coldly.

'You went wrong here,' said Luke, pointing to a particularly complex section of the diagram. 'You need to add an equation into the computer control.'

Luke opened his exercise book and scribbled down an elaborate mathematical formula, littered with strange symbols and complicated fractions. He turned the book so that Carl could read it. 'Yeah?'

'I'll take your word for it,' said the overweight kid.

'Then the power flow stabilises,' continued Luke. 'And all your problems are over.' He sat back in his seat, chuffed with himself.

Jeffrey, whose grin had been growing broader and broader during this, now turned away from the boys. 'You're right,' he said quietly to himself. 'All my problems *are* over.' Then even quieter. 'Don't know about *yours* though...'

Chapter Five

Coldfire Construction

Outside the school gates, Maria and Clyde had seated themselves on a low wall. It was their lunch break, and with all the mouldy food being served in the canteen, they'd brought their own.

Maria was eating some sandwiches her dad had made that morning, while Clyde tucked into a bag of chips. Their friendly silence was broken by the sound of a ringtone.

Reaching into her inside pocket, Maria took out her phone. The display read 'SJS'.

'Hi,' said Maria.

'It's Sarah Jane,' said the voice on the other end. 'I've been to St Cheldon's. It has exactly the same problems as your school. So I'm off to Coldfire Construction.'

'Do you want me to do anything?'

'Yes,' said Sarah Jane. 'Have a look around. See if you can find where that smell's coming from. But remember to be careful!' she added.

'I will,' said Maria. 'See you later. And good luck.'

Maria's mobile folded shut with a satisfying clunk.

'Who was that?' said Clyde.

'Nobody,' lied Maria.

'*Reeeesult!*' announced a proud Mr Jeffrey. He had just shown Luke's equation to the headmaster.

'That's it!' cried Blakeman. 'And he just handed it over?'

'Hilarious!' the science teacher gave a patronising chuckle. 'Humans, eh? Even the clever ones are stupid!'

'At last – we will be avenged!' Blakeman's eyes had taken on a demonic glow. 'We'll finish this puny planet!' A wicked smile curled the edges of his mouth. 'And we'll finish it *tonight!*'

Sarah Jane turned her car around a corner into an industrial estate near Isleworth. There was nothing out of the ordinary about the area. It was drab, grey and depressing, much like a 1,000 similar estates dotted on the outskirts of towns and cities all over the country.

She drove slowly along the winding access road, taking in the numbers of the units as she passed. Then she slowed to a stop. Unit 113.

Leaving her car, Sarah headed along a cracked concrete path that led to the front door. On the wall was a tarnished plaque offering the name of the company. Coldfire Construction.

Miss Smith raised a hand, ready to knock on the riveted metal door, but she noticed it was ajar. She pushed it fully open and stepped inside.

A dingy, chilly entrance hall, smelling metallic and damp, was the first thing that greeted her. The concrete floor was covered in crates filled with old newspapers and boxes of odds and ends. A calendar from the previous year showing photographs of fluffy kittens hung skew-whiff on one wall. In a corner, a fridge stood with its door wide open, but no light on inside.

Sarah crept forward, her eyes darting to and fro, taking it all in. Then, all of a sudden, a door at the other end of the passage was flung open and the bulky shape of a woman almost completely filled the frame.

'Can I help you?' barked the stranger.

The day was over for Park Vale School. The pupils were filing cheerfully through the playground and out into the street – more than ready for an evening of freedom.

Luke couldn't help smiling when he spotted Maria heading in his direction. A friendly face at last. He got up from where he'd been squatting reading a textbook and signalled to her.

'Someone looks happy,' she said. 'I had double maths this afternoon.'

'Science Club was brilliant.' Luke was dying to tell her all about it. 'Mr Jeffrey's nice. I think we're going to be friends.'

Maria frowned. 'You don't make friends with a teacher.'

'Why not?'

'You just don't,' she replied. 'Anyway, Sarah Jane phoned me. She wants us to look inside the new block. Come on.'

Luke nodded and they started to head back inside.

Just then, Clyde called out to them. 'What are you two doing?' he demanded to know. 'School's over.' He stared at Luke for an answer.

'We've got to investigate the – '

'I left something behind,' interrupted Maria, not wanting Clyde to know what they were up to. And with that she darted into the new building.

Clyde put a hand on Luke's shoulder, halting him in his tracks. 'What is it with you and her?' he asked, frowning. 'I've seen weird people. I *know* weird people. But you two – you're *beyond* weird.'

Luke had had enough of Clyde's sarcasm. 'Go and find some normal people then!' he snapped, and marched off after Maria.

But Clyde wasn't deterred. No sooner had Luke reached the entrance hall than Clyde appeared at his elbow. 'I want answers!' he demanded. 'Where are you from?'

'London,' said Luke. And he continued examining the internal structure of the building. 'The layout doesn't make sense,' he mused to himself.

Clyde pressed ahead with his questioning. 'But where've you been all your life?' He threw his hands in the air in frustration. 'I mean, you don't know farting's funny. You let your mum kiss you in public. Where was your last school?'

'I've never been to school before.'

'Your mum taught you at home?'

'No,' replied Luke. 'And Sarah Jane isn't my mum.' He returned to his thoughts. 'There are sixteen classrooms – '

'Hold on,' interrupted Clyde. 'What's Sarah Jane to you then?'

'She adopted me.'

'Why don't you call her mum?'

'She doesn't want me to.'

'What about your real mum and dad?'

Luke stopped what he was doing and turned to Clyde. 'I haven't got a mother or father.'

Clyde let out a sigh. It was like banging his head against a brick wall.

Luke went back to his calculations. 'This block measures about 1,539 square metres, so double that for both floors...'

'What do you mean?' pursued Clyde. 'Everybody's got a mum and a dad. Even I've got a dad.' He paused. 'Somewhere.'

'But the area of each room doesn't add up to that. So there must be an empty space.' Luke's eyes came to rest on a door, and his face lit up. He had it. 'Through there!' he announced, triumphantly. 'I think you should go home,' he said, turning to Clyde.

But Clyde wasn't going anywhere. He was determined to get to the bottom of this. He stuck close to Luke as he opened the door and went inside...

'So, what are you saying about our company?'

'Miss, er...'

'Call me Janine.'

Sarah had been shown into a pokey, bland

office. It had no windows and was lit by a single striplight, which gave everything a sickly neon tinge. The only furniture was a pair of filing cabinets, and a desk at which Janine now sat. She picked up a sandwich and started to munch on it.

'I've been reading up as much as I could,' said Sarah Jane. 'It's not just these school projects in London. You've moved from country to country, hiring cheap local labour, no questions asked.'

'Oh yeah?' said Janine, between mouthfuls.

Sarah Jane flicked through her notebook until she found the relevant page. 'At your building in Santiago, workers refuse to go in. Food goes off. Endless technical problems.' She paused and looked up. 'Valencia, Paris, the same story. And another thing...' She held up the diagram that Alan had given her. 'The plans for each building have a large empty area behind a wall. Why is that?' Her ever-searching eyes were fixed on Janine's chomping features.

The fat woman put down her sandwich. She was beginning to lose her temper with Miss Smith. 'I really wouldn't keep asking these questions,' she said, menacingly, 'if I was you.'

Sarah Jane sized up her opponent. She didn't like to think ill of people, but it was clear that this Janine was a bitter young woman. Over the years, Sarah had been threatened by experts –

the mighty Sutekh, the Giant Spiders of Metebelis Three – so she felt more than equipped to handle a surly secretary from Middlesex.

'I never stop,' she said, defiantly.

Janine's face darkened.

'I think that because these projects are so far apart, nobody connects you with the problems. So you go on and on and – '

'I strongly advise you to leave right now,' yelled Janine, her enormous bosom quivering with rage. 'If you know what's good for you.'

'Was that a threat?' Sarah Jane's voice had a lightness to it, as though she was about to laugh in the woman's face.

'Yes!'

'Do you realise I'm going public with this?'

'No, you aren't,' said Janine.

'What?'

Janine rose from her seat. 'That was your last chance, Miss Smith, to be fair. I *did* warn you.'

And with that she raised both her hands to her forehead.

At first Sarah Jane thought she was adjusting her hair, which seemed an odd thing to do at a moment like this. In fact, she almost started to laugh. But then she saw what the woman was actually doing...

Janine was slowly unzipping her forehead.

And as she did so, an almost blindingly bright blue light was spilling out of her head. At the same time, the neon tube overhead flickered and popped. Now the only light in the room was the dazzling brilliance coming from Janine.

The light was so bright that Sarah Jane had to squeeze her eyelids so tightly they were almost closed. What on Earth was this creature?

Somehow, Janine was growing – swelling in size and changing in shape – as energy fizzed around her. And all the while, she was advancing towards Sarah Jane...

Chapter Six

Escape to danger

Sarah Jane seized the handle of the door. It turned, but the door didn't open. She was locked in.

She rummaged in her bag and grabbed her sonic lipstick. She pulled off the gold lid and extended the device inside. But just as she was about to activate it, a mighty claw smacked it out of her hand and the lipstick clattered to the floor.

Sarah Jane turned around and faced her enemy. For the first time she saw that Janine wasn't Janine anymore, but had transformed into a creature the like of which she'd never seen before – not in all her travels in time and space.

The skin of the woman was lying in a pile on the ground, and instead, towering over Sarah Jane was a huge, reptilian creature.

An alien.

It must have been a squeeze for it to have fitted inside Janine's skin. Big as she was, this monster was larger still – at least eight feet tall.

It had elongated, sinewy arms, nearly trailing on the floor, each ending with an enormous three-fingered hand and razor-sharp talons as long as bread knives. A massive belly flopped down over strong, muscular legs.

The creature threw back its head and opened its small mouth containing rows of razor-sharp teeth. It issued a gurgling, blood-curdling screech.

Sarah Jane gasped in terror, but she didn't scream.

Sarah Jane never screamed.

Maria edged cautiously down a corridor on the first floor of the new block at Park Vale. She pushed open the door of a classroom and went inside.

A computer lab greeted her. It smelt of fresh paint, and had obviously never been used. Individual desks, each with their own monitor, mouse and keyboard lined the room. Row upon row of them. It was all very bizarre.

As she crossed the room, her foot banged against

a shiny metal dustbin and the room echoed with the clang.

'Who's that?' said a gruff voice. 'Hello?' it called.

Maria did the first thing that came into her head, and hid under a desk.

'I know you're in here.' It was Mr Jeffrey. He entered the room cautiously and sniffed at the air.

Maria remained totally still, holding her breath. The next thing she heard was that now-familiar sound. *Phaaaaarzzze!* The teacher let out a giant gust of hot air, just as his legs came into view alongside Maria's hiding place.

'I can smell you,' he said, threateningly.

He could smell her? Maria couldn't understand it. What did he mean?

'A little girl. Fresh as a daisy. Sugar and spice and all things nice.'

Seeing that his feet were now pointing away from her, Maria took a sneaky peek at Jeffrey, who was scanning the room, his nose in the air.

'She really shouldn't be hanging around school after home time,' he chuckled. 'Not when I've got no reason to hide in this stupid skin any longer.' Jeffrey let another belly-shaker of a fart. *Phaaaaarzzze!* 'Because, after all, why should I hide?'

Reaching up, Jeffrey slowly unzipped his

head and pulled back the skin. A dazzling light flooded the classroom. Maria stared in horror as the creature slowly peeled down Mr Jeffrey's skin like sliding the wrapper off a chocolate bar.

The Bane had been terrifying enough, but this was even worse. How many different kinds of aliens were there in London? This thing had been squeezed inside the former teacher all this time. Right under everyone's nose.

'I am Slitheen!' came the hoarse, vibrating cry of Kist Magg Thek Lutovia Day Slitheen.

Maria froze. It was only her second day at Park Vale and now it looked as if she'd never live to see a third. But then, slowly, she regained her nerve. It wouldn't be long before the alien sniffed her out, so she bolted for the door.

Kist span round. 'I love it when they run!' he cried.

'There's another room,' said Luke, pointing to a blank wall at the end of a corridor. 'A secret room.' They had arrived at a dead end, which was odd for an otherwise conventional building like this. 'It must be behind there,' he added. 'But how do we get inside?'

'What?' said Clyde, shaking his head in disbelief. 'There's nothing there! It's just a wall!' He turned to Luke and gripped him by the shoulders. 'Stop...

being...*strange!'*

With that, Clyde turned and marched off down the corridor. Luke looked after him, but he didn't follow. He had to get into this mysterious, hidden room and find out what was going on in Park Vale.

He failed to notice the tiny whirr of a CCTV camera high on the wall behind him...

Sarah Jane had jammed herself between a wall and a filing cabinet, just out of the creature's line of vision.

The Slitheen – whose real name was not Janine but Florm Rox Rey Fenerill Slam Slitheen – padded carefully around the room, sniffing as she went. She was trying to locate the direction of the human aroma that floated in the air.

She had a baby-like face now she had assumed her true form. She was almost cute. But her cold, uncaring eyes revealed her true nature. Sadistic. Heartless.

'I know you're in here,' called Florm, in her alien staccato. 'I can smell you.' She sniffed again. 'What lovely perfume you're wearing, Miss Smith. You're positively fragrant.'

Sarah Jane stayed still, trying not to breathe.

In the capacitor room, an amused Mr Blakeman watched a frightened Luke on his scanner screen. He had his mobile phone pressed to one ear.

'Your Luke Smith's too clever by half,' he said. 'He's right outside.'

'There's another one,' replied Kist, the Slitheen who had been hiding inside Mr Jeffrey's skin. 'I'm after her now.' He sounded out of breath. 'Oh, it feels good. After so long.'

'Rejoice in your hunt, brother!' boomed the head, triumphantly. And he let out a cruel, childish laugh.

Maria raced down the stairs and out into the foyer at the back of the new block. There was no exit here. Just then, Clyde appeared from another corridor.

'We're outta here!' shouted Maria. 'Come on!'

'What?'

'Where's Luke?'

A voice echoed around the foyer. 'You're out there, girl,' it said.

Maria turned white with horror.

'It's only Mr Jeffrey,' said Clyde, noticing his friend's reaction.

'Oh, and there's another one,' said Kist. 'A boy!'

There was the sound of slow, heavy footsteps

coming from along the corridor. And the sound was getting ever closer.

'You're sad,' laughed Clyde, smugly. 'Hiding from a teacher. What's he gonna do – give you detention?'

Just then a deafening roar filled the air. Clyde and Maria span round to see the vast form of Kist Slitheen, his arms raised in attack.

'Whoa, no!' howled Clyde. And the pair ran for their lives.

Luke stared intently at the blank wall. It's a door, he said to himself. And every door must have a handle.

He moved his hand slowly across the surface, feeling for any change. He felt something – more like the tingle of an electrical current than anything physical. 'About here.' He stopped, and pressed into the wall.

Where there was once nothing, an edge appeared and a small, rectangular section of the wall moved inwards with a low clunking sound.

Luke stood back as the entire wall began to slowly slide across. He had opened the door. But what lay inside?

Maria and Clyde raced down the corridor as fast as their legs would carry them.

Behind them, the Slitheen was in hot pursuit. Its long legs took huge, exaggerated leaps forward, and its arms helped propel it with enormous force. For such a large creature, its movement was almost graceful – like a cheetah chasing a gazelle.

'Run as fast as you can, kiddywinks! I'm coming to find you!' screamed Kist, loving every second of the chase.

Maria took a look over her shoulder. The alien was gaining on them. She grabbed Clyde by the arm and they turned suddenly up a flight of stairs. The Slitheen didn't notice, and bounded on down the corridor.

All Sarah Jane could see from behind the filing cabinet was a fraction of the room. At the moment she was perfectly happy about that. At least she couldn't see that hideous creature.

The room had momentarily fallen silent. Perhaps the alien had got bored, Sarah Jane thought to herself. Or perhaps it had changed into some other ghastly incarnation.

Just then, the worst thing that could possibly happen, happened.

The face of the alien loomed right into Sarah Jane's own. She gagged as it exhaled a stinking, rotten breath.

'Run!' screamed the Slitheen. 'It's no fun if you don't run!' And with that, it smashed the filing cabinet – Sarah Jane's only protection – to one side like a matchbox.

'The smell of human fear,' roared Florm. 'Love it!'

Maria and Clyde had paused on the first landing. They gazed down over the edge of the balcony at the floor below. The Slitheen came loping into view, sniffing the air. For a moment, they could do nothing but stare at the alien below.

'We've gotta get out,' whispered Maria.

'We can't,' replied Clyde. 'We need to fight it.'

Behind them a classroom door opened. The kids held their breath, terrified at what they might see...

They sighed with relief. It was only Carl – the chubby kid they remembered seeing in the canteen the previous day.

'Quick!' he called. 'In here.'

Maria and Clyde followed him into the classroom.

Luke entered the secret room. It was filled with all kinds of alien technology, like nothing he had ever imagined. In the middle stood six torpedo-like structures, pointing skywards. They towered above

Luke, crackling and sparking with mysterious power.

Just then, Mr Blakeman appeared from behind this massive device. Luke took a step backwards.

'So, Luke,' said the headmaster, in a relaxed and cheery tone. 'How do you like our little science project?'

'Where's Jeffrey?' asked Clyde, once they were safely inside the classroom. 'I heard him.'

'*That's* Jeffrey!' insisted Maria. 'The thing chasing us.'

Clyde was resigned. 'Oh, I'll believe it. Why not?'

'Thanks,' said Maria, turning to Carl. 'Is there a way out through here?'

'No,' replied Carl. He smiled a chubby smile. 'There's no way out.' It was then that Maria noticed the boy's voice was changing from bored adolescent to sinister villain. 'You see...' He let out a long, high-pitched exhalation of gas. *Phaaaaarzzze!*

'No!' gasped Maria. She guessed what was coming next.

Carl began to unzip his forehead. Blue light blazed out as the rest of the room seemed to darken. Then the child pulled down the skin that covered his head, as a disgusting green form struggled out.

There were fizzing, crackling sounds and, as the skin suit was lowered, another smaller Slitheen stood before Maria and Clyde.

The thing spoke. Slowly and menacingly. 'I am a child of the Slitheen!' it gurgled.

Carl was gone, but before them stood a creature from their darkest nightmares.

It raised its mighty claws, ready to kill...

Chapter Seven

Sarah Jane to the rescue

Clyde and Maria both realised they had just one slim chance of escape. The Slitheen child was blocking the only exit from the room – they had to get past him.

The creature, whose true name was Korst Gogg Thek, advanced on them. Then Clyde seized his chance.

Quick as lightning, he reached to the side, grabbed a chair and flung it into the monster's path. The Slitheen stumbled. 'Run!' yelled Clyde.

The pair darted around either side of the alien

and flung open the door.

They were out!

'Come on, boy,' teased Blakeman. 'Don't you want a closer look?'

Luke stared into the headmaster's flashing eyes, as he advanced on him. Then, seizing his chance, he raced out of the secret room. He may not have known much about life, but he knew when he was in danger.

Luke activated the door mechanism, it slid shut, trapping Blakeman firmly inside. He sprinted away down the corridor.

The stairs flew past under their feet as Clyde and Maria pelted down to the ground floor of the new block. They were in another corridor. There was a door leading to the outside at the end of it.

Suddenly, Luke flew round a corner and nearly cannoned into them. 'There's a secret door,' he panted.

'Not now!' hissed Maria.

The Slitheen child's voice pierced the air. 'You're never getting out of here!' he hissed.

The three kids ran to the door and Clyde wrenched at it.

'Get it open!' yelled Luke, panicked.

'It's locked!' said Clyde. 'That thing is real, isn't

it?' No one replied. 'It's *real*,' he repeated, as if trying to convince himself.

'This place is sealed,' laughed Korst, the boy Slitheen. 'You're finished! Right here, right now!'

'This way!' called Maria and tore off.

Just then, Korst appeared from a side corridor, cutting the boys off from Maria, who'd sailed on ahead of them. He roared furiously. They had no choice but to spin round and retrace their steps.

'Maria!' Luke called back plaintively over his shoulder.

'Come on!' shouted Clyde.

They had no choice but to abandon their friend...

'Good sense of smell, have you?' asked Sarah Jane, looking fearlessly back into the face of Florm Slitheen, while at the same time rummaging through her handbag.

'Oh, yes,' breathed Florm. 'Best nostrils in the galaxy. And that's official!'

'And you like my perfume?' asked Sarah Jane, lightly.

'Lovely...'

Sarah Jane pulled out a small bottle of scent. It was neither sonic nor alien. It was from Boots. 'Then sniff this!' she shouted, and pumped several squirts into the air.

Florm span backwards, coughing violently.

'It's cheap, but it's not *that* bad,' chuckled Sarah Jane, and smashed the entire bottle onto the floor.

The room filled with a suffocatingly sweet smell. Florm's eyes began to blink frantically, water streaming down her face. She tried to use her giant hands to wipe the scent away, but this only made it worse, causing the creature to issue a shrill wail.

Now the danger had temporarily passed, Sarah Jane bent down and retrieved her sonic lipstick. She activated the device. *Vreeeee!*

The door of the office popped open.

Sarah Jane ran across the entrance hall, out of the building and dived into her car. Revving the engine, she sped away.

After taking one deep breath to steady her nerves, she put her mobile into its cradle on the dashboard and speed-dialled Luke's number. 'I was wrong,' said Sarah Jane, when he answered. 'It *is* aliens.'

'I know!' came Luke's gasped reply. And then Sarah Jane's blood ran cold as she heard the terrible sound of a Slitheen roar.

'You too?' she wailed. 'Right, listen! You've got to...'

Luke snapped his phone shut. 'Make a smell!' he shouted. Clyde looked baffled.

They were running down a corridor. Kist, the Slitheen who'd been living inside Mr Jeffrey, was in hot pursuit.

'Sarah Jane says their sense of smell is very sensitive. Make a big enough smell and we can get away.'

'What are you saying?' panted Clyde. 'We should fart our way out?'

'Would that be funny?'

'Come out, little ones!' said Kist, in a sing-song tone.

Then another voice joined in. 'They're nearby, Daddy,' it said. 'I can smell you, new Luke.'

'We need a strong smell,' urged Clyde.

'A skunk?' asked Luke.

'Where're we gonna find a skunk in west London?'

Clyde and Luke stopped running and pushed themselves flat against the wall. Clyde quickly rummaged in his bag and pulled out a can of deodorant. He held it up for his friend to see.

'Wolverine,' said an out-of-breath Luke, reading the label. 'Pure masculine action.' He smirked.

'What?' said Clyde, a little offended.

'That's funny.' Luke was proud of himself. He was starting to get it.

Suddenly, the two Slitheen, father and son, appeared round the corner. Korst, the child, let out a triumphant scream – then they advanced...

Clyde sprayed his deodorant into the air. The aliens clutched their faces. They choked on the scent and staggered backwards.

'Go!' shouted Clyde.

The two boys tore off down the corridor.

Sarah Jane's car came to a skidding halt outside the gates of Park Vale School. She flung the door open and raced towards the new block.

Before she saw them, she could hear their hammering. Clyde and Luke were banging their fists against the plateglass doors. But they couldn't open them.

Maria joined them. 'Think we've lost them,' she said.

'Behind you!' yelled Sarah Jane, spotting two Slitheen approaching from the rear. 'Get back!'

The kids moved away from the doors as Sarah used her sonic lipstick to unlock them.

Luke, Maria and Clyde burst out of the building.

Sarah reversed the setting on the device and the doors slammed back shut, automatically locking themselves with a solid clunk.

And not a second too soon, as just then the

two Slitheen and Mr Blakeman crashed into the exit. But they were unable to get out. All three pounded on the doors.

'Into the car!' instructed Sarah.

As they ran for the car, Clyde turned to her. 'What's that?' he asked.

'Sonic lipstick,' she replied, matter-of-factly.

'Of course.' Clyde shrugged.

'What's he doing here?' she asked Maria.

'Sorry.'

'Somebody else's life in my hands. Just what I needed.' Sarah Jane sounded exasperated.

All four of them clambered into her car, Sarah Jane started the engine and they sped off.

Having given up trying to open the doors, Kist, Korst and the headmaster stared after them as they drove away.

'That's not fair, Daddy!' moaned the child, petulantly. 'That woman cheated! I want my hunt!'

His father put a massive arm around the lad. 'Come here,' he said, and gave the boy a reassuring squeeze.

'That woman had some sort of sonic disruptor,' said Blakeman. 'This is a level five planet. They're primitives. How did she get that? Who is she?' he demanded.

'The galactic police? She could be one of their agents,' offered Kist.

'No. She's human. She smelt... soupy. Like they all do.' Blakeman dismissed his concerns. 'Still, if that's her only weapon, she's no big deal.' He turned and moved off.

'Daddy,' said Korst. 'I want to hunt! Why do I never get what I want?'

From an early age the Slitheen are taught to embrace the pursuit and slaughter of other creatures. While on Earth, humans were their prey.

'You'll have your hunt, I promise,' his father replied. 'After all, tonight's the night the lights go out...'

Chapter Eight

Luke's big mistake

S arah Jane Smith's car had never been so full. She felt like a school bus driver instead of a journalist. How had all these children managed to get caught up in her crazy life?

Aliens were one thing, she thought – but three kids? That was ridiculous.

'I want answers!' demanded Clyde, as they all piled out of the car in front of Sarah's house. 'I've just been chased by aliens. *You* weren't even freaked out. Why? Who *are* you lot?'

'You've gotta go home – forget this ever happened,' insisted Maria.

'No! I'm gonna find out the truth,' replied Clyde,

firmly. 'I'm part of this now. What's in *there*?' He pointed at Sarah Jane's house. 'Who's that *woman*?' He pointed at Sarah Jane herself. 'What's going *on*?' He pointed at nothing and everything at the same time.

'Leave us alone!' shouted Maria, and she moved off towards number thirteen. She was only doing this for his own good, to protect him – but Clyde didn't see it that way.

He produced his mobile. 'The police won't leave you alone, though, when I tell them what just happened.'

Maria stopped and slowly turned around. He had her there.

Blakeman and Kist Slitheen arrived at the blank wall that disguised the entrance to the capacitor room.

'At last,' said the headmaster. 'We've waited so long for this moment. Think about it.'

Kist sighed. 'Times have been hard.'

'They've been closing in on us from all sides. The other families against us. Judoon forcing us out.' He was referring to the freelance galactic police, infamous for their use of extreme force. 'We've been exiles. But this will give us a new beginning. Wealth, security –'

'When we have the money – what then?' interrupted Kist.

'We'll buy a fleet of battle cruisers and return home to Raxacoricofallapatorius.' That was their home planet, on which the Slitheen family – for they were a family not a species – were convicted criminals sentenced to death.

'I shall smite the Grand Council, crush the Senate!' continued Blakeman. 'The Blathereen and the Hostrozeen will beg for mercy at my feet! And then I'll...'

Blakeman loosened his collar. He was becoming agitated at the thought of how he would humiliate the other families back home, who had all betrayed and spurned the great Slitheen clan.

'But I mustn't get carried away,' he said. 'First things first. We have the equation. Nothing can stop us.'

He activated the secret door. It slowly retracted, revealing the interior of the capacitor room.

'Now it begins!'

'Inhabitants of Raxa...Raxa...Oh, blimey!' Sarah Jane was in her attic reading from the display of her scanner watch. She was having trouble with the pronunciation.

Luke peered over her shoulder. 'Raxacoricofallapatorius,' he said, with a grin.

'Thanks.' She continued reading. 'The outcast Slitheen family are scavengers, thieves of others' technology, known to infiltrate low-tech planets by hiding in the skins of the dominant native species.' Sarah Jane paused. 'Slitheens in Downing Street,' she muttered.

'What?' asked Luke.

'Something a friend said once.' She recalled what Rose Tyler had said to her when they were at another school, battling the Krillitane.

Had these Slitheen been responsible for the destruction of Number Ten Downing Street a couple of years ago? The media had said the alien ship that landed in the river Thames had been a hoax. Sarah Jane smiled ruefully to herself. She knew better than to believe everything the newspapers said.

She continued reading from her watch. 'Gas exchange from body compression often results in... Oh!' She stopped.

'Farting?' offered Luke. 'Farting is funny.'

Sarah looked up. Maria and Clyde had entered the room.

'Right, what's going on here?' asked the boy.

'Why not bring all your little friends round? The whole school!' said Sarah, crossly.

'If he tells anybody, who's gonna believe him?' offered Maria.

'Wait, wait, wait!' Clyde was in need of some attention. 'I've just had monsters from outer space on my back. No one's telling me what's going on.'

'Just shut up for a moment, I'm busy!' Sarah Jane's bark was enough to silence him. 'Right now, you're not important. Huh! It's getting like Clapham Junction in here.'

Sarah Jane needed time to think. Her young friends looked up at her expectantly.

'Right,' she continued at last. 'The Slitheen must have taken over Coldfire Construction. They've thrown up buildings all around the world. But why?'

Maria and Clyde just shrugged, but Luke looked shamefaced. 'I think I might know,' he said, with a nervous edge to his voice. 'There's a hidden room in the school. I saw inside.'

Maria was eager to hear. 'What was in there?'

'I've got a theory about it.' Luke paused. 'Mr Smith could help...'

'Who's that?' sneered Clyde. 'Your dad?'

It was at times like these that Sarah Jane would have turned to K-9 for help. But he was busy sealing off a black hole caused by Swiss scientists, and had been for the past eighteen months.

'Mr Smith,' called Sarah. 'I need you.'

Clyde span round to where a clicking, whirring noise was coming from. The lights in the attic flashed on and off, and the brick chimney breast started to divide and slowly open up.